Leila, Chirpy and the Story-Writing Competition

Story by Diana Noonan

Illustrations by Sumiti Collina

Contents

Chapter 1

Butterflies

It was Monday morning. Leila was upstairs in her bedroom, getting ready for school. She made her bed and put her piano music into her backpack. Then she ran downstairs and skipped excitedly into the kitchen.

Her brother, Akeem, and her little sister, Maryam, were already sitting at the table eating their breakfast. Mum was at the bench, making their lunches for school and for work. Chirpy, the family's cheeky green parrot, was flying in and out of the kitchen through the door that led to his aviary.

“I can’t wait to get to school!” Leila told everyone. “Today, Ms Layton is going to tell our class how to enter our school’s new story-writing competition.”

“That sounds exciting,” said Mum.

“It is!” said Leila, who loved writing stories. “I’m so excited about the competition, I have butterflies in my stomach!”

“Chirpy’s excited, too,” said Akeem, as Chirpy let out a loud screech.

Chirpy flew around and around the kitchen and landed on Akeem's shoulder.

"Good morning, Chirpy," said Akeem.

"Good morning! Good morning!" shrieked Chirpy.

"Clever Chirpy!" giggled Maryam.

Mum put a little dish of chopped fruit and vegetables on the window ledge. "Here's your breakfast, Chirpy," she said, as Chirpy flew over to eat it.

"Don't forget to eat *your* breakfast, Leila," said Mum, putting some warm bread on Leila's plate.

But Leila felt too excited to eat. All she could think about was the story-writing competition, and what the rules might be.

"Whose turn is it to fill Chirpy's water dish?" asked Mum, looking into Chirpy's aviary.

"Mine," said Akeem.

"Hurry up, then," said Mum. "And fill it right to the top. It's going to be a very hot day."

Mum looked at Leila. "Make sure you check that Akeem has closed the door to the aviary when he's finished in there," she said.

Leila sighed. She was the oldest child in the family, so it was her job to check that Chirpy was safely locked in his aviary every morning.

"I won't forget," she told Mum.

After breakfast, Akeem went into the aviary to fill Chirpy's water dish. Chirpy followed closely behind him.

Leila went upstairs to get her backpack and clean her teeth, but she was still so excited about the story-writing competition that she forgot to put toothpaste on her brush!

"Hurry up, Leila!" called Mum from downstairs. "It's time to leave for school. We're waiting for you."

Leila rushed downstairs and out to the car. She wished the butterflies would stop fluttering in her stomach.

Chapter 2

An Empty Head

Leila and Akeem hopped out of the car at the school gate.

"Don't forget about your piano lesson with Ms Ho after school," said Mum to Leila. "She'll bring you home as usual when it's over."

"I won't," said Leila, as she waved goodbye to Mum.

Leila ran all the way to her classroom, and slid into her seat between her best friends, Alissa and Jessa. Ms Layton was standing at the front of the room.

"Good morning, everyone," Ms Layton said. "I hope you all had an enjoyable weekend, and that you're feeling full of fresh ideas to use in our story-writing competition."

Leila's heart went thump, thump, thump. It was so loud, she glanced sideways at Alissa and Jessa to see if they could hear it, but they were looking straight ahead at Ms Layton.

"The reason we're having the competition," said Ms Layton, "is because a past pupil of the school, who is now an author, suggested it. His name is Mr Wagner, and he's donated book vouchers for the prizes."

"Book vouchers!" Leila whispered to herself, as the butterflies in her stomach fluttered faster than ever.

"And the best news of all," said Ms Layton, smiling, "is that your stories can be about anything at all! There is no special topic. The choice is yours."

Everyone started talking at once, and Ms Layton had to tap on the whiteboard to ask for quiet.

"You have all of today and tonight to think about your story ideas," said Ms Layton. "Tomorrow morning, in class time, you will write your stories."

For the rest of the morning, all Leila could think about was the competition. But at break time, her excitement turned to worry.

As Leila sat under the trees with her friends, it seemed that everyone had a story idea except for her. Her friends were excited to share their story ideas, but the butterflies in Leila's stomach started fluttering again.

Alissa said her story was going to be about the time she and her mum got stuck in a lift.

Jessa said she was going to write about her cat coming home after being missing for three years. Jessa's twin brother, George, said he was going to make up a story about a spaceship that landed on their lawn.

But the more Leila listened to everyone else's cool story ideas, the more she just couldn't think up one of her own.

If only my butterflies would go away, she thought, *I'd be able to think properly.*

At the end of the school day, Leila was so worried about not having a story idea that she went to see Ms Layton.

"I think you might be worrying too much about it," said Ms Layton, kindly. "Try not to think about the competition for a while, and I'm sure an idea will just pop into your head."

I hope so, thought Leila, miserably, as she walked towards Ms Ho's house for her piano lesson. *Because, right now, my head feels empty!*

Chapter 3

Escape

After the piano lesson, Ms Ho drove Leila home. Leila tried hard to smile as she thanked her, but she still felt worried. Even though Leila had done her best to concentrate on her piano playing, a story idea *still* hadn't popped into her head. And the excited butterflies in her stomach had turned into a tight, uncomfortable feeling.

Leila opened the front door and went to the kitchen to find Mum. But before she got there, she heard loud voices coming from the backyard.

Leila ran through the kitchen and out the back door. Mum and Maryam were standing on the lawn below the big peach tree that grew beside the garage. Leila thought they were looking up at all the ripe fruit, but then she heard Akeem shouting. His voice was coming from the tree.

"I can see him!" Akeem called. "He's pecking a peach!"

"Come down!" called Mum to Akeem. "I don't want you up there in the tree. It's not safe."

"It's Chirpy," said Mum, when she saw Leila. "The door to his aviary was left open this morning. He must have flown into the house and escaped through an open window."

"Akeem's in the tree," added Maryam. "He's trying to catch Chirpy."

Leila suddenly remembered that she hadn't checked the door to Chirpy's aviary before she left that morning. She'd been too busy thinking about the story-writing competition. She wanted to cry, but she knew she had to keep calm if they were going to catch the little parrot.

"I'll go and get Chirpy's seed dish," Leila told Mum. "If I rattle the seeds, he might come down for some."

"Good idea, Leila," said Mum. "We need to catch Chirpy before your brother hurts himself."

As Chirpy hopped from branch to branch above him, Akeem climbed higher.

"Akeem!" called Mum, again. "*Please* come out of the tree before you fall!"

Maryam reached for Leila's hand. "Will Chirpy come back?" she asked quietly.

Leila looked down at Maryam, who was trembling with worry. "Of course he will," said Leila, as brightly as she could. But inside, she didn't feel so sure.

"I'm just one branch away from him, now," Leila heard Akeem say as she ran back into the house for the seed.

Inside, she rushed to the aviary and picked up Chirpy's seed dish, then ran back out onto the lawn with it. But just as Leila reached Mum and Maryam, the branches of the peach tree shook wildly, and Akeem landed on the ground below them with a loud thump.

"Akeem!" cried Mum, rushing over to him. "Akeem, are you okay?"

Leila and Maryam ran over to Akeem, too. Maryam started to cry.

"My ankle hurts," wailed Akeem.

Mum tried to help him up, but Akeem said his ankle was too sore to move.

"I'm going to call an ambulance," Mum said, reaching into her pocket for her phone. "Don't move, Akeem!"

As Mum began to tap the screen of her phone, Leila saw a movement out of the corner of her eye. It was Chirpy! He'd flown onto the roof of the garage and was looking down at them.

"Come here, Chirpy," said Leila, rattling the seed dish over the sound of Akeem's whimpering. "Good little bird. Come to Leila. Come on!"

Chapter 4

Gotcha!

Akeem sat on the grass below the peach tree, holding his ankle. Mum went to get an umbrella to hold over him because it was so hot.

As they all waited for the ambulance to arrive, Leila walked quietly towards the garage, where Chirpy was still on the roof. She held out the dish of birdseed and shook it gently. The seeds rattled, and Chirpy tilted his head to one side, as though he was listening.

"Come on," coaxed Leila, "come and get your yummy birdseed, Chirpy."

Chirpy strutted towards the very edge of the roof and ruffled his feathers. As Leila rattled the seed once more, he peered down at her from the roof's edge. Before she had time to do it again, Chirpy spread his wings and glided down to land on the lawn, just a step away from her.

Behind her, Leila heard Maryam gasp.

"Shh," said Mum quietly to Maryam.

"Come on, Chirpy," whispered Leila. "Come and have some seed."

Very quietly, Leila got down on her hands and knees. She put the seed dish on the grass in front of her. Chirpy looked at the dish suspiciously, then hopped towards it. Leila moved forward a little.

But Chirpy was too smart to be caught that way. He stepped back and began talking. "Clever bird, clever bird," he chirped. "Tea time, tea time, hello Chirpy, good boy, good boy!" he said.

In the distance, Leila heard the sound of an ambulance siren. From next door, the neighbour's dog began barking, and suddenly, Chirpy stopped talking. He stretched out his neck and looked behind him. And in that moment, Leila reached out her hand and grabbed the only part of Chirpy she could – his tail!

For an instant, she was afraid the tail feather she was holding between her fingers might come loose, and Chirpy would escape. But the feather held firm until Leila was able to get a better hold on him.

"Gotcha!" she cried.

By now, the ambulance was in the driveway, and two paramedics in uniform were hurrying across the grass towards Akeem. One of the paramedics shone a small light in Akeem's eyes, and the other gently felt his leg.

"We'll need to take Akeem to hospital so a doctor can check his ankle," one of the paramedics told Mum.

"You're welcome to come in the ambulance with him," added the other paramedic, but Mum explained that there was no one at home to look after Leila and Maryam.

"It's okay. We'll follow behind in the car," Mum told her.

"Quick!" said Mum to Leila and Maryam as the paramedics began gently lifting Akeem onto a stretcher. "You two hop into the car while I lock the house."

As Mum turned the car to follow the ambulance along the road, Chirpy began to cheep softly.

"He sounds quite happy," said Leila.

"Oh, dear," said Mum to Leila. "I didn't realise Chirpy was with us. Why didn't you put him in his aviary?"

"You told us to get into the car," said Leila. "Besides, I wanted to check that he was okay. We don't know how long he's been outside. Another bird might have attacked him!"

Mum sighed loudly. "I don't know what you're going to do with him while we're at the hospital," she said. "You can't leave him in the car in this heat."

Leila looked at Chirpy. She didn't know what she was going to do with him, either.

Chapter 5

Chirpy the Entertainer

Mum drove into the hospital car park. "Stay where you are for a minute," she told Leila and Maryam. "I think I have something we can put Chirpy in that will keep him safe."

Leila heard the car boot open and close. Then she saw Mum standing beside the door with a square zip-up grocery bag. Mum opened Leila's door and passed the bag to her.

"Put Chirpy in this bag, and zip it closed," she told Leila.

"He won't like going in there," said Leila.

"It's the best we can do," said Mum. "At least he won't escape when we take him into the hospital waiting room."

Leila carefully put Chirpy into the bag and zipped it up.

Inside the hospital, the waiting room was nice and cool. Mum spoke to the woman at reception. Then she told Leila and Maryam to sit in the waiting room while she went to find Akeem.

"Stay together," Mum told them. "If you need anything, the woman at reception will help you. If you need me, ask her to call my phone."

To begin with, Chirpy was silent, but after a while he began to chatter to himself inside the grocery bag.

At first it was quiet chatter, but when Leila didn't open the bag, Chirpy got louder and louder. Then he gave several shrill screeches.

"Shh!" said Leila against the side of the bag, but it was no good, and now everyone in the waiting room was looking at her. The receptionist came over.

"Do you have a bird in that bag?" the receptionist asked Leila.

Leila felt her face go red. She wished Mum would come back. She craned her head to look for her, but she couldn't see her anywhere. So Leila found herself explaining to the receptionist everything that had happened.

"And we can't leave him in the car, because it's too hot," Leila finished.

"He would probably be happier in a cage," said the receptionist, kindly. "I know that the aged-care home next door has one. They use it to take the home's pet cat to the vet for its check-ups. I'll ask someone to fetch it."

A little while later, the receptionist brought the cat cage over to Leila. It was the perfect size for a small parrot. Chirpy could see out of it, and it even had a little dish clipped to the inside, which the receptionist had filled with water. Chirpy seemed pleased as he explored his new cage.

Leila and Maryam were delighted. The receptionist had been so kind to them, and the cage was perfect for Chirpy. As Leila let out a sigh of relief, Chirpy took a good, long drink, and started talking again.

"Hello, hello! Who's a pretty birdie?" he chirped. "Cup of tea!"

Chirpy sang and chatted happily, and by the time Mum came back, almost everyone in the waiting room had gathered around to listen to him.

"He's a lot of fun," said the receptionist to Mum. "I wish we could keep him!"

"You're welcome to him," laughed Mum. "He's the reason we're here!"

Mum told Leila that the nurses thought Akeem had a sprained ankle. But because the hospital was very busy, it would be quite a while before a doctor could see him.

Then, Mum went to the hospital cafe. When she came back, she had sandwiches for Leila and Maryam, and a packet of toasted sunflower seeds for Chirpy.

"They'll make him chirpier than ever!" said Leila, as Chirpy began pecking at the seeds.

Mum smiled. "I don't think anyone will mind," she said.

Chapter 6

Now That's an Idea!

It was almost dark by the time Mum drove everyone home from the hospital. Akeem used his new crutches to hop out of the car and into the house. Mum carried a sleepy Maryam up to her room and put her to bed. Leila carried Chirpy into his aviary in his borrowed cat cage and let him out. It wasn't until she had closed the door behind him that she suddenly remembered about the story-writing competition the next day.

"I still don't have an idea for the story-writing competition!" Leila said, in a panic, as Mum came into the kitchen. "There's been no time to think of one. What am I going to do?"

"Didn't you say you are allowed to write about anything?" asked Mum, thoughtfully. "Isn't that right?"

"Yes," said Leila, "but I can't think of anything special. I've never been stuck in a lift like Alissa and her mum. I've never had a cat that was lost for three years and then came home – that's what happened to Jessa."

Mum looked closely at Leila. "But you *did* have a pet parrot that escaped, and a brother who fell out of a tree trying to catch it."

Leila's mouth fell open in surprise. "I guess I did!" she exclaimed. "And I *did* catch the parrot by its tail!'

"*And* take it to the hospital!" laughed Mum.

"*And* put it in a cat cage when I got there!"

"*And* it entertained everyone in the hospital waiting room," said Mum.

Leila's mind began filling with ideas. "What if a TV reporter was in the hospital waiting room, and heard the parrot talking, and asked its owner if she would go on TV with it?" gasped Leila. "Wouldn't that be cool!"

"I don't think you're going to have any problem at all thinking of ideas for your story," said Mum, laughing. "Now go to bed so you're wide awake to write tomorrow morning."

Leila ran upstairs and got into bed as fast as she could. Her mind was racing with ideas for her story. She couldn't wait for the competition to start tomorrow.

Chapter 7

The Long Wait

The next morning in class, Leila wrote like she'd never written before. The words came effortlessly, and by the time Ms Layton said, "Time's up!", Leila knew it was probably the best story she had ever written. But would it be good enough to win the competition? She would have to wait until Friday to find out. That was when the school principal, Ms Parata, would announce the winners at a special assembly at the end of the day.

That week, Leila took over Akeem's turns at cleaning Chirpy's water dish because it was too hard for Akeem to get into the aviary on his crutches. Chirpy was on his best behaviour.

"I think he knows he shouldn't have escaped," said Leila at breakfast, when Chirpy flew onto her shoulder after she called him.

On Friday morning, Mum's phone rang just as everyone was leaving for school. Mum didn't say much to whoever was calling, but Leila heard her reply, "I see. Yes, that's fine. I'll be there."

"I've got butterflies in my stomach again," said Leila, as Mum drove the car to school. "It's because we find out the winners of the story-writing competition at the end of the day, at a special assembly."

"You haven't got *too* long to wait, now," was all that Mum said.

That afternoon, Leila walked to the school hall with Alissa and Jessa. When all the children were seated, Ms Parata walked in with a tall, grey-haired man.

"This is Mr Wagner," Ms Parata told the assembly. "Mr Wagner is an author, and he has donated the prizes for the story-writing competition."

Ms Parata then began announcing the winners. There was one winner from each class. Ms Parata started with the younger students, and worked her way up to Leila's class.

"In Ms Layton's class, we have two equal-first winners," said Ms Parata.

Leila held her breath. She scrunched her toes up in her shoes and looked down at the floor.

"They are Jessa Tomkins," said Ms Parata, "and Leila Osman."

Leila let out her breath in one big rush. Everyone began clapping as she and Jessa stood up and walked side by side onto the stage.

"Jessa wrote a very interesting story about her pet cat," said Ms Parata, "and Leila wrote a most unusual story about a parrot that went to hospital!"

Mr Wagner shook the girls' hands and handed them each an envelope. Then he leaned over and said something to Leila that made her want to giggle out loud.

As she walked off the stage, holding in the giggle, she was astonished to see Mum, Akeem and Maryam right down the back of the hall, waving to her.

After assembly, they were all waiting for Leila near the school gate.

"Was it Ms Layton who called you this morning?" Leila asked Mum.

"Yes," said Mum. "She called to invite us all to the assembly. But she said it was a secret!"

At home, Leila sat at the table with Akeem and Maryam, eating an after-school snack. Chirpy was perched on her shoulder.

Suddenly, Leila felt like giggling again.

"Do you know what Mr Wagner said to me?" she asked Mum.

"What did he say?" replied Mum.

"He said my story about Chirpy felt so real he wondered if it might actually be true!"

Maryam and Akeem started giggling.

Leila and Mum started to laugh, too.

And Chirpy let out a *very* loud screech!